WHER TAS AND BEC?

94

KNOWLEDGE BOOKS

© Knowledge Books and Software

MASTERY DECODABLES

In the garden there is a gate.

Tas likes to sit by the gate.

The gate is always shut.

The gate is big.

Bec can sit on the gate.

Tas can not sit on the gate.

Tas can not open the gate.

Oh no! Can you see?

The gate is open.

Who did not shut the gate?

Where is Bec?

Where is Tas?

Gem can see the gate is open.

Bec is not in the shed and Tas is not on the mat.

Gem looks for Tas.

Gem looks for Tas by the tree.

Gem looks for Tas by the pile of rocks.

Gem looks for Tas by the water pipe.

Gem looks and looks.

What can she do?